DANIIL KHARMS

FIRST, SECOND

Translated from the Russian by Richard Pevear

Pictures by
MARC ROSENTHAL

Farrar, Straus and Giroux
New York

Published simultaneously in Canada
by HarperCollins*CanadaLtd*
Color separations by Prestige Graphics
Printed and bound in the United States of America by Worzalla
Designed by Lilian Rosenstreich
First edition, 1996

Library of Congress Cataloging-in-Publication Data
Kharms, Daniil, 1905-1942.
[Vo pervykh i vo vtorykh. English]
First, second / Daniil Kharms ; translated from the Russian by Richard Pevear;
pictures by Marc Rosenthal. — 1st ed.
p. cm.
[1. Counting.] I. Pevear, Richard. II. Rosenthal, Marc, ill. III. Title.
PZ7.K52655Fi 1996 [E]—dc20 94-44128 CIP AC

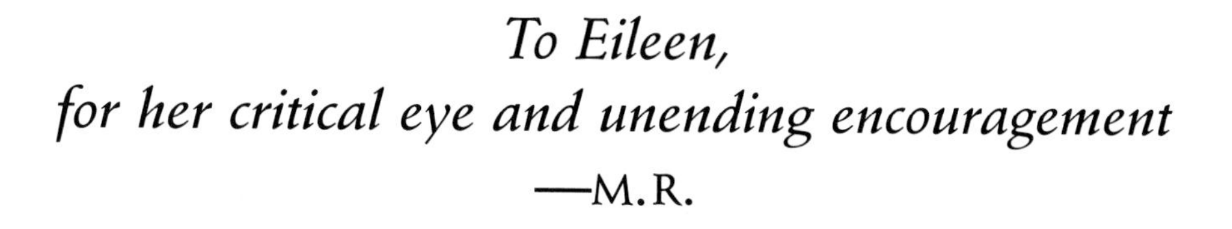

To Eileen,
for her critical eye and unending encouragement
—M.R.

FIRST,

I stepped out singing a song.

CONCERT
Prof. Willy
VOTE FOR BECKY DUNN

SECOND, Pete came up and said, "I'm going with you." And we both went along singing songs.

THIRD, as we went along, we saw a man no bigger than a jug standing in the road.

"Who are you?" we asked.

"I'm the shortest man in the world," he said.

"Come with us," we said.

"All right," he said.

And we all went along. But the short man couldn't keep up with us. He ran as fast as he could, but he still fell behind. Then we took him by his hands: Pete took the right hand and I took the left. The short man hung between us with his feet barely touching the ground. And we went on, all three of us, whistling songs.

EXPRESS

FOURTH, we went along like that and what did we see but a man lying by the side of the road. His head was propped on a stump, and he was so long that we couldn't see his feet. We came closer and he jumped up and hit the stump once with his fist and pounded it into the ground.

Then the long man looked around, saw us, and said, "Who are you to go waking me up?"

"We are three merry fellows," we said. "Do you want to come with us?"

"All right," said the long man, and he took one step and went twenty yards.

"Hey," shouted the short man, "wait for us!"

We grabbed the short man and ran after the long one.

"No," we said, "you can't walk like that. Take little steps."

The long man started taking little steps, but it was no use. Ten steps and he was out of sight.

"Okay," we said, "let the short man sit on your shoulder and take one of us under each arm."

The long man put the short man on his shoulder, took us under his arms, and we all went on.

"Are you comfortable?" I asked Pete.

"Very. And you?"

"I'm comfortable, too."

We began whistling merry songs. The long man walked along whistling songs, and the short man sat on his shoulder whistling for all he was worth.

FIFTH, we went on and what did we see but a donkey standing right in our way. We cheered and decided to ride the donkey. The long man tried first. He threw his leg over the donkey's back, but the donkey didn't even come up to his knee. The long man was just sitting down when the donkey up and walked away, and the long man sat full force on the ground. Then we tried to put the short man on the donkey. But the donkey had gone only a few steps when the short man lost his balance and fell off. He got up and said, "Let the long man carry me on his shoulder again, and you and Pete ride the donkey."

We did as the short man said and were all happy and went along whistling songs.

SIXTH, we came to a big lake. There was a boat on the shore.

"Let's get into the boat," said Pete.

The boat was just right for Pete and me, but we had some trouble with the long man. He had to sit all doubled up with his nose between his knees.

The short man sat under one of the seats, but there was no room at all for the donkey. If the long man had not been in the boat, there would have been room for the donkey. But both of them were too much.

"You know what?" said the short man. "If you, the long man, wade across the lake, then we can take the donkey in the boat and there will be room for all of us."

So we took the donkey aboard, and the long man waded across the lake, pulling our boat behind him on a rope. The donkey sat, afraid to move. Maybe it was his first time in a boat. But the rest of us were happy, and we went along in the boat whistling songs. The long man whistled songs, too, as he pulled us across the lake.

SEVENTH, we climbed out on the other shore, and there sat a car.

"What might this be?" asked the long man.

"What's this?" asked the short man.

"This," I said, "is a car."

"A car in which we are about to go for a ride," said Pete.

We began to settle ourselves down in the car.

Pete and I sat in the front seat, the short man climbed on the hood, but for the long man, the donkey, and the boat there was not enough room.

If we put the boat in the back seat and the donkey in the boat, it would have been all right, except that there was no place to put the long man.

If we put the long man in the boat, there was no place for the donkey.

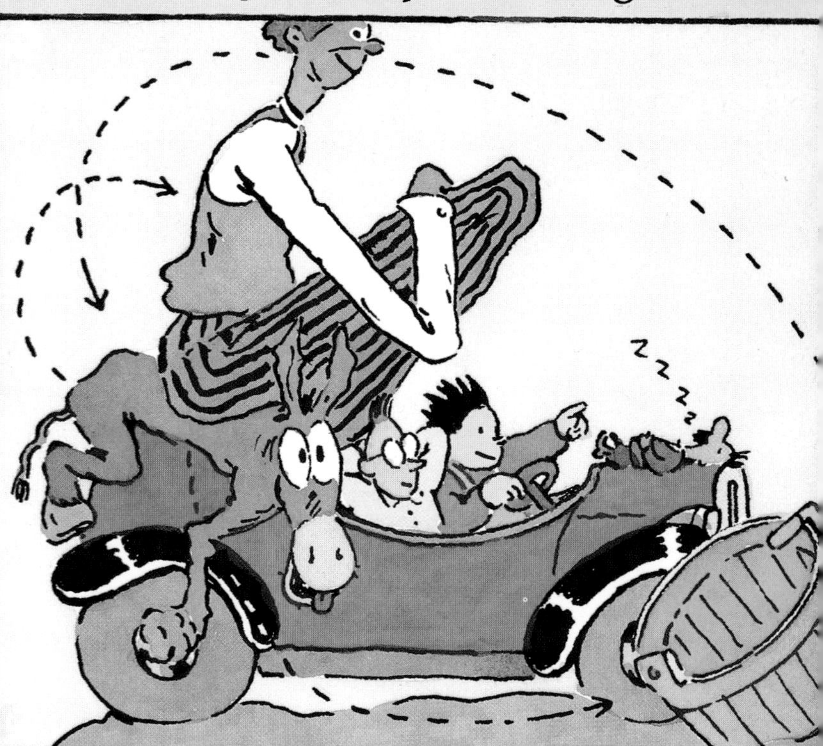

If we put the long man and the donkey in the back seat, there was no room for the boat.

We had no idea what to do. But the short man gave us some advice.

"Let the long man sit in the back seat," he said, "and let the donkey lie on his lap, and he can hold the boat up over his head." So the long man got into the back seat, and we put the donkey on his lap and gave him the boat, which he held up over his head.

"Is it heavy?" asked the short man.

"No, it's okay," said the long man.

I started the car and off we went. And everyone was happy, except for the short man, who wasn't very comfortable on the hood. He bounced around like a roly-poly. But the rest of us were fine, and we drove along whistling songs.

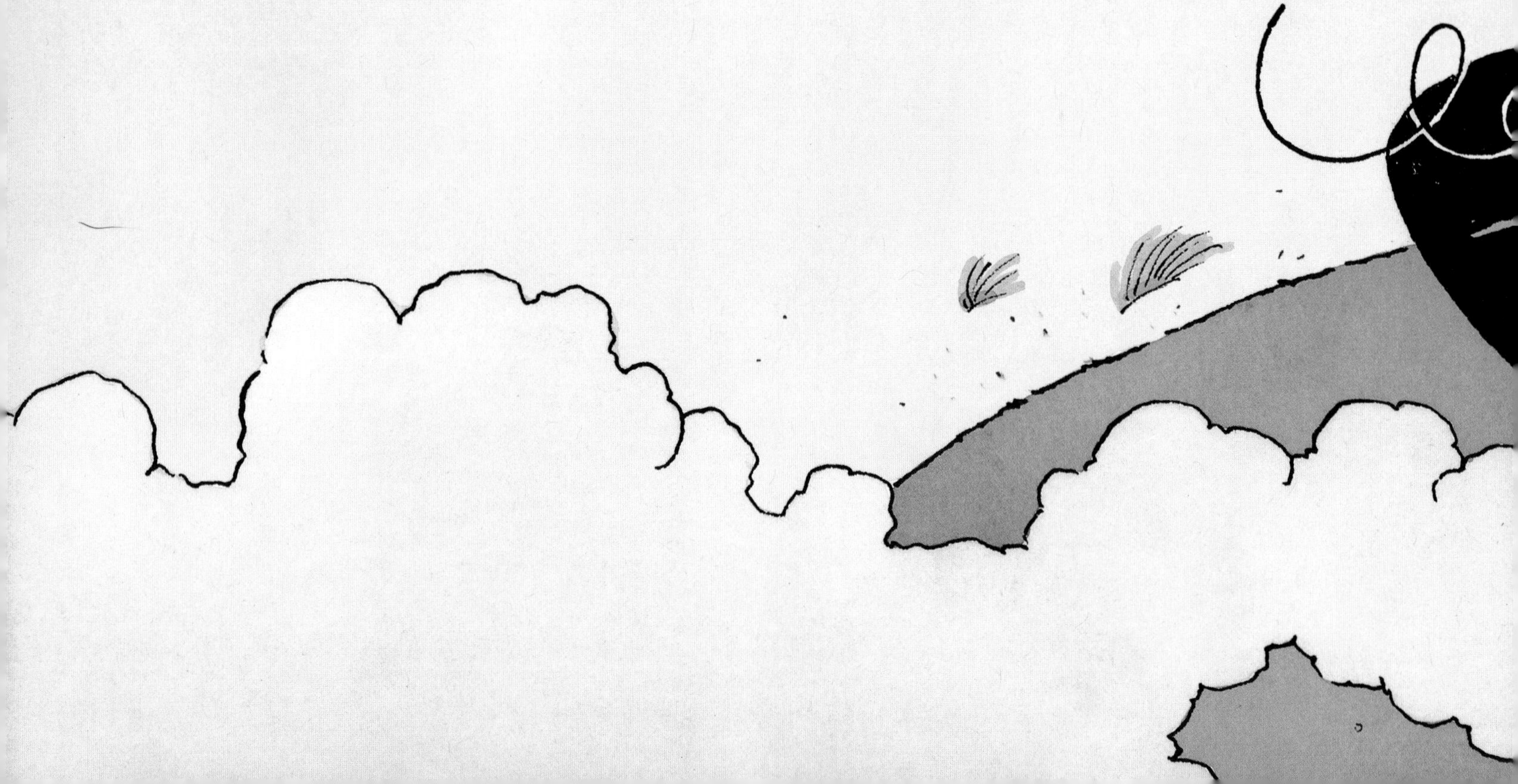

ZIPPY'S
EXPRESS
ACME
ARTHUR

[illegible], we came to a town. As we drove down the street, people stared at us and pointed their fingers. "Look at that," they said. "A big oaf sitting in a car with a donkey on his lap and a boat over his head! Ha, ha, ha! And the one on the hood! No bigger than a jug! Look how he's bouncing around! Ha, ha, ha!"

We drove straight up to an inn, set the boat on the ground, put the car in the garage, tied the donkey to a tree, and called for the innkeeper. The innkeeper came out and said, "May I help you?"

"Listen," we said to him, "would you mind if we spent the night here?"

"Not at all," said the innkeeper, and he showed us to a room with four beds.

Pete and I went to bed, but the long man and the short man couldn't make themselves comfortable. All the beds were too short for the long man, and the short man couldn't put his head on the pillow because the pillow was taller than he was, and all he could do was lean against it. But we were all so tired that we finally worked things out. The long man simply stretched out on the floor, and the short man crawled up onto a pillow and fell asleep there.

z z Z Z Z Z Z
Z Z Z
?

NINTH, we woke up the next morning and decided to go on our way.

Then all of a sudden the short man said, "You know what? I've had enough of dragging this boat around, and I've had enough of this car. Let's go on foot."

"I'm not going by foot," said the long man. "I'll get too tired."

"You, such a big, strong fellow, will get tired?"

"Of course I'll get tired," said the long man. "I just wish I could find the right-sized horse."

"Where will you find the right-sized horse?" Pete interrupted. "You don't need a horse, you need an elephant."

"And you won't find any elephants around here," I said. "This isn't Africa."

Just as I said it, we heard a lot of shouting and barking outside. We looked out the window and saw an elephant walking down the street, with a crowd of people following him. A little dog ran between his feet barking with all his might, but the elephant walked calmly on without paying any attention to anyone.

"Well," the short man said to the long man, "there's your elephant. Get on him and ride."

"And you ride the little dog. He's just the right size for you," said the long man.

"Right," I said. "The long man can ride the elephant, the short man can ride the little dog, and Pete and I will ride the donkey." And we all ran out to the street.

INN

TENTH, we ran out to the street. Pete and I got on the donkey, the short man stayed by the gate, and the long man ran after the elephant. When he caught up with the elephant, he jumped on it, turned around, and came back to us. The little dog ran after the elephant, barking with all his might. As they reached the gate, the short man took careful aim and leaped on the little dog's back. And we all rode away: first the long man on his elephant, then Pete and I on the donkey, and last the short man riding on the little dog. We were all happy and were whistling songs.

MALCOLM'S
MAGIC PILL

We left the town and rode on our way. But where we went and what happened to us next is another story.